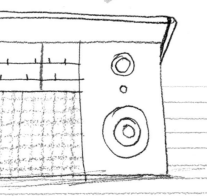

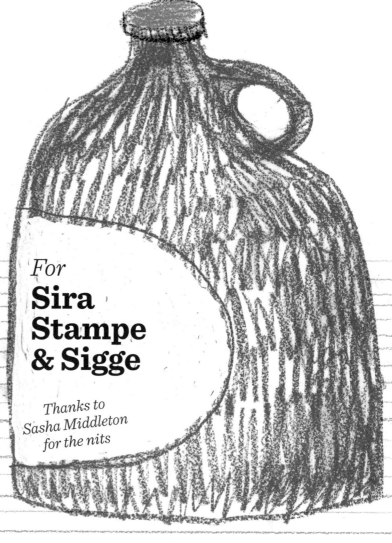

For
**Sira
Stampe
& Sigge**

*Thanks to
Sasha Middleton
for the nits*

Library of Congress Cataloging-in-Publication Data

Mackintosh, David, author, illustrator.
Lucky / by David Mackintosh.
pages cm

Summary: When Leo's mother announces
there will be a surprise at dinner, Leo
and his brother are desperate to find
out what it is, and their imaginations
run wild.
ISBN 978-1-4197-0809-1
[1. Surprise—Fiction.] I. Title.
PZ7.M2167Lu 2014
[E]—dc23
2013044957

First published in hardcover in Great Britain by HarperCollins Children's Books in 2014. HarperCollins Children's Books is a division of HarperCollins Publishers Ltd.

Text and illustrations copyright © David Mackintosh 2014
Book designed and lettered by David Mackintosh

Printed and bound in China   10 9 8 7 6 5 4 3 2 1

Abrams Books for Young Readers are available at special discounts when purchased in quantity for premiums and promotions as well as fundraising or educational use. Special editions can also be created to specification. For details, contact specialsales@abramsbooks.com or the address below.

ABRAMS
THE ART OF BOOKS SINCE 1949
115 West 18th Street
New York, NY 10011
www.abramsbooks.com

LUCKY

David Mackintosh

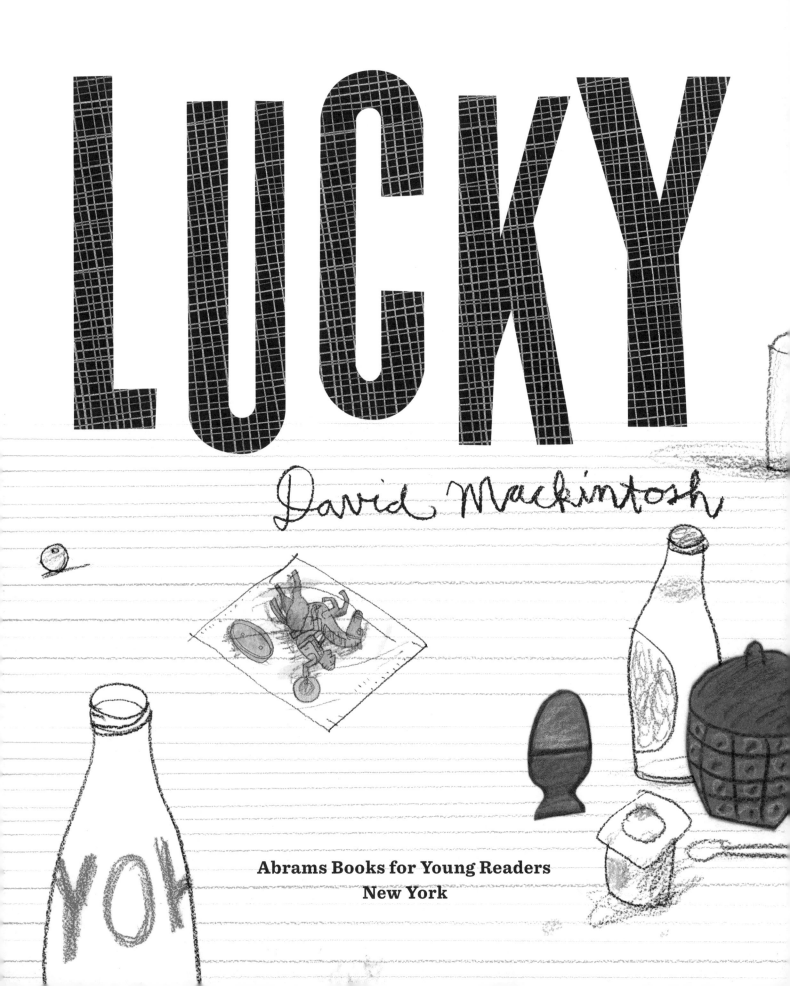

Abrams Books for Young Readers
New York

We're having a surprise at dinner tonight. Mom says so.

"WHAT IS IT?!"
my brother asks.

"Just wait and see,"
says Mom.

My brother, Leo,
thinks it's curly
fries.

But
I start
thinking . . .

Last time we had a surprise,
I got a new bike.
Well . . . it won't be a new bike.

"*Yeah*, it's not your birthday," says Leo.

It must be even better than that.

Hey! Maybe it's tickets to
the Amazing Yo-Yo Super Show
at the town hall.

"Dad *said* we could go!"
my brother shouts.

But the Super Show finished
last week. *Phooey.*

Maybe it's a brand-new car!
My brother thinks our old
one smells funny.

Hmmm.
Dad likes our car.
He always washes it.

I have
an idea . . .

MAYBE

WE'RE GETTING A

SWIMMING POOL

IN

the backyard.

"We'll need chlorine and earplugs *too*," Leo says.

But we live in a high apartment and don't have a back-yard.

So that can't be it.

Hey . . . we might be getting an elevator!

But Mom says that climbing stairs is good for our calves.

Just maybe . . . my very own room,

so I won't have to share with Leo for one second more.

But I doubt it. It took Dad forever to even put in the doggy door for Abraham.

I   GIVE   UP.

I try
to
think of
something
that
will
take my
mind
off
guessing
what the
surprise
will
be.

Then
I start
to think
that
there
won't
be a
surprise
at all.

Sometimes
grown-ups say
things they don't
really mean.

This could be
one of those times.

Today, we have our eye exam
with School Nurse Karen.

That's when Leo says,

"HEY!
I bet we're going to
Hawaii for two weeks:
all expenses paid!"

Leo says,

In Hawaii, you drive around in golf carts and have spending money and drinks with fruit in them.

***And...** There are erupting volcanoes there, with rivers of boiling lava and clouds of rotten-egg gas.*

***Plus...** To protect against volcanoes and falling coconuts, people wear grass skirts and flower necklaces and strum tiny guitars called ukuleles.*

But Hawaii looks expensive . . . We usually stay at home watching TV and arguing on holidays.

So . . .

MOM AND DAD MUST HAVE WON THE VACATION IN A CONTEST!

Maybe Leo IS right: We ARE going to Hawaii for two weeks!

**On the field trip,
I tell Lance Campbell,**

who tells
Melody Diaz,

who tells
Penny Kurtz,

who tells
Sheldon Robe,

who tells
Hani Sherbet,

who tells
Bernard Joy,

who tells
Honey Garrett,

who tells
Felicity Singh

**that my family
has won a
contest
to fly to Hawaii
for two weeks.**

"All expenses paid," adds Leo.

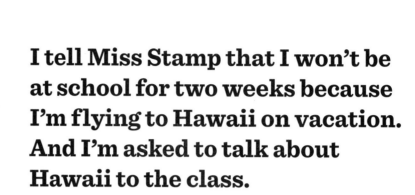

I tell Miss Stamp that I won't be at school for two weeks because I'm flying to Hawaii on vacation. And I'm asked to talk about Hawaii to the class.

Afterward, the principal says that this is the first time in history that anyone from our school has ever won a vacation.

PUPIL OF THE DAY.

To celebrate,
we're all given
ten minutes of free time.

After school, me and my brother rush home, faster than ever.

"Let's get a milk shake from Giorgio's!" Leo yells.

No. No time for milk shakes.

"Are you going to watch *Jumpy Jim?*" he puffs.

No time for TV. We need plenty of time to pack our stuff for Hawaii, and we'll be catching a plane.

Dad once told me,
You can't be late for planes.

When we get there,
I tell Mom that SHE'LL be
surprised because me and
Leo have already guessed
what the—

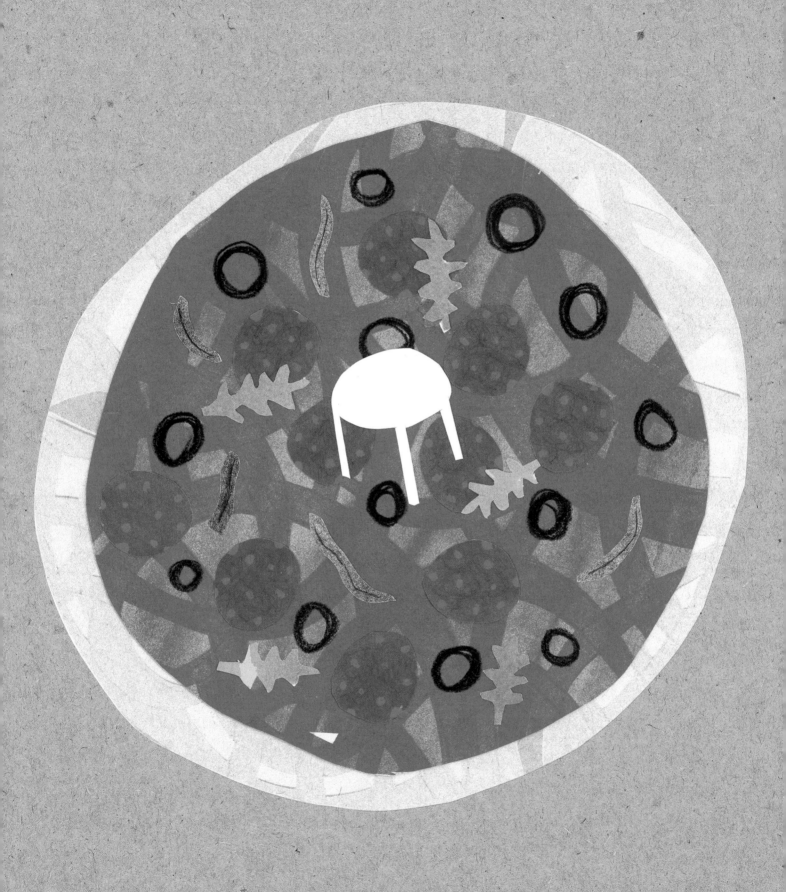

"PIZZA!" shouts Mom.

"WOO-HOO!" shouts Leo.

Pizza? *Pizza?*
I ask if she's sure
the surprise isn't
two weeks in
Hawaii because
she won a contest
on the radio.

Hawaii? *Hawaii?*
Mom laughs and
slices the pizza
with a little
wheel.

I don't feel very hungry,
so I go to my room for a while.

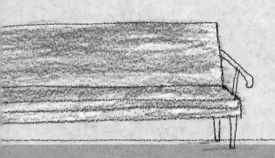

I can hear Leo blabbing about
what happened at school
today. Especially the part
about Hawaii and how we all
got free time outside.

Mom is laughing, and Dad
makes a loud snorting noise
like a horse. Then *he* begins
laughing, and I can hear him
playing Leo's stupid guitar.

*What will I tell Miss Stamp
tomorrow?*

Soon, Leo is at the door. But I'm still not hungry.

"**Come on—it's a *different* surprise.**"

"It's Hawaiian Pizza!"
shouts Leo.

Then he calls our banana
splits Hawaiian Ice Cream.

Sometimes, Leo makes
my whole family laugh.
Including me. And I don't
even *like* pineapple.

He's good like that.

But I still don't want to share a room with him.